HIS WILLING CAPTIVE

MEN OF THE SEA BOOK THREE

SADIE KING

HIS WILLING CAPTIVE

Have you ever wanted something so much you'd do anything to get it?

That's how I feel when I see Layla. All innocence and sunshine against my darkness.

My whole life I've taken what I want, and I don't let anything get in my way.

So, I take Layla.

But getting her on my yacht was only half the battle.

Now I have two days to convince her to stay, or I lose her forever.

But she must never find out what I did to get her on my boat…

His Willing Captive is a kidnapping, instalove romance featuring an OTT obsessed man who will stop at nothing to claim his curvy woman.

LET'S BE BESTIES!

A few times a month I send out an email with new releases, special deals and sneak peeks of what I'm working on. If you want to get on the list I'd love to meet you!

You'll even get a free short and steamy romance when you join.

Sign up here:
www.authorsadieking.com/free

1

SAILOR

The motor vibrates under my hand as I guide the tender to shore. I'm not sure which back-water bay I've washed up at, but I need supplies before I head on down the coast to Mexico.

Just a quick stop—I don't like to be on land for too long—then I'll be back on the yacht and back to the open sea.

As I approach the jetty, I scan the row of shops and businesses nestled on the shorefront. I'm looking for groceries, a butcher, and liquor.

A woman comes out of the bakery carrying a brown paper bag. My breath catches in my throat, and my heart stops beating.

She's fucking beautiful.

The sun sparkles off her golden hair that hangs in thick waves over her shoulders.

Her too tight t-shirt shows off a first-class rack, large youthful breasts, and wide hips that sway as she walks.

My blood thunders in my ears, heat floods my veins, and my cock hardens instantly.

Mine.

The word runs over and over in my mind as I watch the curvy beauty carry her bag of bread to a bicycle leaning against the wall. A fucking bicycle with an old-fashioned basket on the front. Fucking adorable.

She puts the bags in the basket and mounts the bike before heading down the street.

Fuck.

There's a docking area on the side of the jetty, and I pull in too fast, causing my tender to knock against the pilings. Water splashes over the side, but I've already leapt out and I'm tying off.

Striding down the jetty, I catch sight of my beauty going into the grocery shop.

I'm a man used to getting what he wants. And I want her.

I'm waiting for her when she comes out of the grocery store a little while later, her tanned arms laden with shopping bags.

"Let me help you."

She starts at the sound of my voice. Her clear blue eyes lock on mine, and I swear to God there's a bolt of electricity that shoots between us.

Her mouth pops open at the sight of me. And I don't blame her.

I'm six foot three and broad-shouldered with a rugged beard and ink down my arms. There was a time when I was clean shaven and kept my tats hidden under a tailored suit. But those days are long gone.

The woman recovers from her surprise and regards me with a cool look.

"I can manage."

So, my beauty has some independence. I like that. Still, I'm not the type of man to take no for an answer.

Before she can protest, I grab the shopping bag that's balancing on the top of the pile.

Her brow furrows. "I said I can manage."

"And I said I want to help."

Her eyes regard me intensely, but I'm the master of intense. I return her stare until she looks down.

"I'm Sailor."

The woman puts her bags in the basket of the bicycle and starts wheeling it down the street. "I don't care who you are or what you want, Sailor. I'm not interested."

I let her stride off in front of me, using the opportunity to run my eyes down her back to the generous hips that sway from side to side, making her skirt swish around her ankles.

She's walking ahead of me, but she has no idea that she's already mine. That I'll do anything it takes to make that so.

"What's your name?"

The woman ignores me and keeps walking. I should back off. I should let her be. But there's a deliberate sway to her hips that makes me think that, despite her protests, she likes my attention. Besides, she could cycle off if she really wanted to get some distance instead of pushing the bike.

The woman turns up an alleyway with a bright mural painted on the wall. To my surprise, she slows down, allowing me to catch up with her.

"My name's Layla."

"Layla." I roll the name along my tongue. Sweet as honey.

Layla stops walking and leans her bike against the wall. Her gaze sweeps over my body, and I see a heat in her eyes that matches my own. God damn, this woman was meant for me. I know it in my bones.

"My brother's in the Coast Guard."

She says it like it explains something, and if I'm honest, it's not the best news. I've spent the last several months avoiding the Coast Guard.

"If he sees me walking with a strange man, he'll flip."

So that explains the cold attitude on the waterfront. "I'll make sure he doesn't see us."

She's backed against the wall, and I take a step closer so I can smell her sticky lip balm and salty scent.

Her eyes widen, and the look she gives me sends a bolt all the way to my dick. Her tongue darts out to lick her lips. I follow it with my eyes. Plump lips. Lips I want to bite and suck and feel wrapped around my cock.

"Thanks for helping me with the shopping." She darts away from me and grabs the handlebars of the bike. "My place is just up the road."

I follow her up the alleyway, grocery bags in hand. She turns left onto a row of houses and pushes open the fence to a small cottage.

"Is your brother home?"

I hesitate on the pavement. The last thing I want to do is meet the local Coast Guard.

Layla shakes her head. "No. You want to come in for some coffee?"

In the afternoon sun, her hair shimmers. She's half turned to face me, standing shyly under a cherry tree ripe with swollen fruit. The picture of innocence.

She has no idea how I'm about to ruin her.

2

LAYLA

My heart's thundering in my chest as I push open the front door to the house I share with my controlling brother and my sister, whenever she's home from college.

I've never done anything like invite a strange man home before. But there's something about the rough seaman with the silver-streaked beard that makes me want to do dangerous things.

If my brother knew I'd invited a strange man into the house, he'd kill me. He takes his responsibility for me and my sister very seriously. Too seriously.

Sailor has to stoop to get in the door, and his head scrapes the wooden beams of the ceiling. It's an original fisherman's cottage from the nineteenth century, complete with old stonework, low ceilings, and thick wooden doors. It was made for a time when men were shorter, not like the giant Sailor, who's making my knees weak just looking at him.

Sailor puts the groceries down on the kitchen table, and I start unpacking them. His intense gaze follows me around the kitchen.

"What are you doing in Temptation Bay?" I ask.

He takes a seat and puts his hands together, resting them on the table.

"I came for you."

The words send a thrill down my spine and all the way to my core, even though it's a ridiculous thing to say since I only met him five minutes ago.

I raise my eyebrows. I'm not going to get sucked in by some corny line.

"I bet you say that to all the girls in all the bays you stop at."

Sailor eyes me intensely. "No. I've never said it before."

I snort laugh because, yeah, sure. Like this hot older man has come here especially for me. I don't even know him.

Although I have invited him into my house and feel oddly comfortable with him.

"You want some coffee?"

He nods, and I get to work making it. The whole time as I move around the kitchen, I feel Sailor's eyes on me.

My skin burns under his gaze, and my hands tremble so much I almost spill the coffee.

"What do you do here, Layla?" His voice is gravelly and deep. I could listen to it all day.

"Not much at the moment."

It's kind of true. My sister's the smart one. She's in her final year of law school. My brother's the responsible one. He's in the Coast Guard. Which leaves me, the grunt. I clean the house and buy the groceries and cook the meals. Like a housewife, except I'm nobody's wife.

Sailor must hear the longing in my voice because he tilts his head and regards me with curiosity. "What would you like to do?"

"Now that's a good question."

I set two coffee mugs on the table and take a seat opposite Sailor. He pulls a hip flask out of his pocket and holds it up.

"Go on then." I nod, and he pours a generous amount into the coffee.

"Do you ever feel like there's something more for you out there, but you don't know what it is?"

He leans forward and nods slowly. "I've felt that."

"Like Temptation Bay isn't where I'm meant to be, but I don't know how to leave."

I take a swig of coffee and almost choke on the strong whiskey.

Sailor smiles. "You get used to it."

I don't know if it's the spiked coffee or the intense way he's looking at me, like I'm the most interesting thing in the world, but I find myself opening up to Sailor. To this stranger that I met less than an hour ago.

We talk. Or at least I talk and he listens.

I tell him about my life here, my overprotective brother Andrew, and my sister Coraline, who's coming to visit in a few days.

I refill the coffee, and he adds more whiskey. The room starts to blur. I notice a swirling pattern in his eyes.

I laugh too loud.

He leans closer, and I lean toward him. Our lips meet, and the kiss sends a zing of energy through my body.

When I sit back, the room is spinning, and then I pass out.

My head feels like there's a hammer banging against my skull. I sit up and whack my head on something, which makes it worse.

I'm not in my bed. That much is clear by the cupboard that's above the bed. Squinting around the room, it seems I'm in some kind of cabin.

Through the fog in my head, I try to piece together what happened last night. I remember talking with Sailor. I remember having coffee laced with whiskey. I remember his intense eyes as we got closer and the sting of his lips when we kissed.

Oh God, the kiss. I press my fingers to my lips, trying to feel the warmth still there.

The room rocks from side to side, and there's the sound of water slapping against wood.

I'm on a boat.

The knowledge makes me sit up quickly, this time avoiding the low cupboard, which I can see now is an efficient use of limited space.

I must have gone to Sailor's boat at some point last night.

My heart quickens, wondering what else I can't remember. Tentatively, I slide a hand down to my pants. The buttons are done up. Nothing seems out of order.

Which is a relief. I'm attracted to the man, but I'd like to remember my first time.

My head throbs as I pull myself upright.

I've got no idea what the time is, but my brother will be wondering where I am. There's a load of laundry that needs doing, and I need to clean the house before Coraline arrives.

Pushing the door of the cabin open, I peer out. I'm in a short corridor. There's another door on this side and two adjacent.

Sailor's got a big boat if there're this many cabins. I vaguely wonder where in the marina he was able to park a vessel this size. He's probably anchored it in the bay somewhere, which means we would have left in his tender last night, something else I can't remember.

There's no one around, so I make my way to the stairs at the end of the corridor and climb up on deck.

Sailor is sitting in a comfy chair reading, and he looks up

when he sees me. I'm struck again by how good he looks, with his salt-and-pepper beard and sharp eyes.

"Good morning." He seems more relaxed on the water, more at home.

He's regarding me curiously, a half-smile on his face that makes me wonder again if anything happened last night.

"Morning," I say as I climb the final stairs and step out onto the deck.

I'm disoriented for a moment. I'm looking out to the ocean, which means the bay must be behind me. But I can't see Rabbit Island, which should be on the horizon.

Turning around, my stomach drops. There's open ocean behind me too.

I spin around, my eyes wide, looking for Temptation Bay, looking for home. But around me is nothing but ocean.

My mouth drops open, and my eyes find Sailor's, which are dancing with amusement. "Where are we?"

His mouth twitches into a smile. "We're at the start of your new life."

3

SAILOR

Confusion sweeps over Layla's face when she realizes we're on the open water. It wasn't easy stealing her away last night. But I wanted her, and I always get what I want.

"What do you mean?" she splutters.

I put my book down on the table and talk slowly, trying to calm her.

"I mean, Layla, that you're mine. I took you."

She gapes at me, her mouth falling open in a way that makes my cock ache.

"Well take me back." She folds her arms over her heaving chest and fixes me with a fiery look. "I want to go home."

"Do you? From what you told me last night, it seemed you were looking for an escape from your humdrum life. I'm giving you that escape."

She shakes her head. "I didn't mean like this. Take me back, Sailor."

She looks confused and angry, and I suppose it is a shock. I know Layla belongs to me. It's taking her a bit longer to catch up.

I stand up and take a step toward her. Her breathing is shallow, and I'm reminded of the kiss from last night. Her soft mouth pressed against mine. The quiet moan that escaped her lips.

"You belong to me, Layla."

She sticks her chin out, and her hands go to her hips. "I belong in Temptation Bay."

My thumb grazes her defiant chin. She gasps at the contact.

"If you want to go back, then I'll take you back."

Relief floods her eyes, and she visibly relaxes. I sweep a strand of hair off her cheek. "If you still want to get off the boat when we get back to Temptation Bay, you're free to go."

She scoffs at me. "Of course I'll want to get off."

My finger slides down her cheek, down the line of her neck, and trails off at the base of her throat. She takes a sharp intake of breath.

"We'll see."

"Yeah." She steps back quickly, and I'm amused to see I've got her rattled by my touch. "Why the hell would I want to stay with someone who's kidnapped me?"

She turns away and storms back down the stairs. I let her go to give her time to cool off.

I'll set a course back to Temptation Bay, but I'll make it take a day or two.

Now I just need to convince Layla to stay.

4

LAYLA

The door to the cabin slams shut behind me, and I grab the nearest thing I can find, which is a pillow, and throw it on the bed.

Of all the audacious things to do. Who the hell does he think he is to take me like that? The man has some balls.

I just hope he can get me to shore quickly. Then I never have to see him again.

My heart's racing. I try to ignore the tremor I felt when he said I belonged to him.

There're some paperbacks on a shelf in the cabin, and I grab one of them. I'm not going out there again until we're back at the bay.

It's a few hours later when there's a gentle rap on the door. I sit up on my elbows as Sailor pushes the door open and peers in.

His eyes meet mine, and there's an electric bolt between us, a humming that I feel all through my body whenever he looks at me.

Damn him. It's incredibly difficult to stay angry when my body's behaving like I want this man.

"I made you something to eat."

"I'm not hungry." My belly gives a low rumble, giving me away.

"Okay." He gives a half-smile. "If you don't want fresh fish caught this morning, then I guess I'll have to eat it all myself."

My stomach does another growl. Damn it.

"Fine." I clamber off the bed. "But don't expect me to talk to you."

"Oh, I don't expect you to talk." He gives me a wicked grin that makes my insides pool. Then he's gone, and I follow him up onto the deck.

I don't know what I'm expecting, maybe to see the mainland in the distance, but the only land I see is an island I don't recognize on the horizon.

"How far away are we?"

"We'll pull into a bay of the island to shelter for the night, and then we should get you home tomorrow."

"Tomorrow? My sister's arriving today, and my brother will be wondering where I am."

"Don't worry. I left a note."

I squint at him. How can he be so casual about all this? He kidnapped me, yet he's behaving like we're on a date.

"Relax." Sailor indicates one of the seats. "Sit down and eat."

"But I thought we were heading back?"

He slides a plate over to me that's laden with fresh white fish. My stomach growls at the sight of it.

"We are heading back. But the wind's against us, so it's gonna take time."

I eye Sailor suspiciously. How we got out this far in one night, I'll never know. But at least he's taking me back. I may as well eat.

We're on the front deck. Dinner is set around a cream-colored outdoor dining set, and I take a seat on the opposite side of the table from Sailor.

"You caught this?" I hold up the fish and take a bite. It flakes apart in my mouth, the pure taste making me moan.

"Off the back of the boat this morning."

The fish is good, and I eat slowly, savoring the fresh taste. Sailor watches me as we eat, and yeah, I should be angry with him, but I find myself relaxing.

"What do you do out here?" Sailor told me yesterday that he lives on the boat.

"I fish and read and sleep."

"But don't you work?"

He rubs his beard and looks out to the ocean. "I used to, but I don't have to anymore."

"Okaaay."

He's being annoyingly evasive, like he's hiding something. But that's fine. Another day and I'll never have to see him again.

"What do you want to get back for anyway?" he asks.

I think of my life. Washing dishes, folding laundry, listening to Coraline talk about the amazing things she's doing at law school.

"My sister."

He nods slowly. "Are you close?"

"We were, until she went to college. Now I just see her for the holidays."

"We can come back for holidays, Layla. Stay with me on the sea, and we'll come back and visit your sister."

I've finished eating my fish, and I push the plate away. "I thought you were taking me back."

"I am. And I stand by my promise. If we get to Temptation Bay and you still want to leave, you can. But I'm planning on making you want to stay."

"And how on earth are you going to do that?"

For a big man, Sailor moves swiftly. Suddenly he's beside me, grabbing my wrists.

I gasp at his nearness, and the pressure on my wrists sends shivers down my spine.

"If I kidnapped you, shouldn't you be tied up?"

Oh shit. There's a wicked glint in his eye that makes my panties dampen.

Grasping my wrists, he pulls me up to my feet.

"Sailor…"

"I want to show you how I'm gonna make you stay."

He tugs on my wrists and pulls me to the mast standing in the middle of the deck. I stumble after him, half thrilled, half terrified.

My arms are tugged above my head, making my breasts stick out. His eyes flick to them, and his expression darkens.

"What are you doing?"

My voice comes out as a squeak. My throat is dry, and my body's on fire.

"Don't speak, sweetheart."

Sailor takes a thick rope and binds my wrists, tying me to the mast. He gives the rope a tug, making sure my wrists can't come free.

"This is how I'm gonna make you stay."

His mouth is inches from my ear, his hot breath on my throat.

"By tying me up, holding me captive, and keeping me by force?" I can't keep the sarcasm out of my voice.

He pulls his head back and his eyes are dark, intense, and serious. "I don't do anything by force, Layla. If you want me to stop at any time, you tell me to stop."

My breathing's shallow, and I could ask him to untie me, tell him not to breathe on my neck or run his hands over my body.

But I don't.

A smile spreads across his lips. "Good girl."

His hands slide over my neck, and he tucks my hair over my shoulders. His lips glide down my throat, following his hands. His palms glide over my breasts, and I push my chest against him, arching my back, aching for him to touch me.

"This body is mine, Layla."

As he says it, he slides a hand up my top and pushes my bra down. My nipples stand at attention as his thumb grazes over them.

I moan at his touch, my insides pooling at his possessive words.

Then his other hand grabs my top and pulls. The fabric rips, and I gasp at the cool air against my skin.

"I don't have any other clothes."

"You don't need clothes."

He unhooks my bra, and my breasts tumble into his hands.

"This body is mine, Layla. I want you naked so I can take you anytime I like."

The words, so filthy, should make me want to run, but instead they make my core ache with longing. I push my hips against him, feeling his hardness and wanting him to be inside me. In this moment, I'm all his, and he can take me anyway he likes.

He must see the need in my eyes because his hands slide to my jeans. He unbuttons them and pulls them roughly down my legs.

His palm cups my damp panties.

"This pussy is mine, Layla. So long as you're on my boat, it's mine."

His words send wetness spraying out of me, and I moan, rubbing myself against his palm.

"You like that, sweetheart?"

I nod. "Yes."

I long to touch him. I pull at the restraints, but he's bound me too tight. I'm at his mercy, and he knows it.

Sailor drops to his knees and rips my panties off.

"What are you doing?"

"I'm claiming your pussy with my mouth."

Rough hands grab my leg and hoist my thigh over his shoulder. I'm exposed, my pussy wide open, and there's nothing I can do about it.

I gasp in shock just as Sailor closes his warm mouth over my pussy. Waves of hot air press against my sensitive nub. I cry out as his tongue flicks over me, and my eyes roll back into my head.

"Fuck, Sailor."

In response, he slides his tongue inside me. It's like all my nerve endings are on fire. I buck my hips and he pulls me closer, pressing me into his face.

"Fuck, that feels good."

He licks my engorged pussy, and then suddenly he's pulling back. The heat is gone. The pressure that was building subsides.

I open my eyes and look down at Sailor sitting back on his haunches.

"What are you doing?" I can't keep the frustration from my voice, but it only makes him smile.

"What would you like me to do?"

"I'd like, I'd like…" It's hard to say the words. "I'd like you to keep doing what you were doing."

He nods slowly, a wicked grin on his face.

"Say you'll stay with me, and I'll give you what you need."

The audacity of this man is unbelievable. "That's not fair." I writhe, pushing my hips closer to him, but he ducks out of the way.

"Love's not fair, honey."

"Love. Why are you talking about love? I just need you to…"

I don't finish my sentence because his thumb presses against my clit, and I let out a low moan.

"Just need me to what, honey?"

The pressure sends heat coursing through my body. If he can just keep doing that…

"Tell me what you need."

He takes his thumb away, and I whine in frustration. "I need you to keep going, to make me come."

"I'll make you come if you say you'll stay with me,

"That's not fair."

His thumb circles my clit, and I press against him, wanting some release—any release.

"Just one more day, Layla. I'll make you come if you agree to stay one more day."

The pressure of his thumb increases before he takes it away again, making me writhe in frustration.

I suppose it wouldn't be so bad to stay on the boat for one more day, eating fresh seafood and having orgasms.

"Fine," I pant. "One more day."

"Good girl."

He buries his face between my legs as his finger slides into me. The heat from his tongue makes the pressure build, and suddenly I'm over the edge.

I scream out as the orgasm races through me, making my body shake and shattering me into a million pieces. The only thing stopping me from collapsing is the rope holding me to the mast.

Sailor keeps his tongue pressed against me until I stop writhing.

When he sits back, he's got a satisfied look on his face.

I'm panting and trembling as he unties my wrists. But I

don't feel satisfied. Reaching for his belt, I pull him toward me. His hand stops mine.

"Oh no, you don't get to feel my cock yet."

Disappointment must be written all over my face. "But I agreed to stay one more day."

"One orgasm for one day, Layla. You don't get my cock inside you until you realize that we're meant to be together and you're staying on my boat."

I look at him in disbelief. What is this power that this man has over me? It's time to use every tool in my arsenal.

I sink to my knees, lowering my lashes. I stick my breasts out and look up at him coyly.

"I'm a virgin. I want you to pop my cherry."

His hand trembles in mine, and he lets out a low groan. His eyes are hooded with desire.

"I will pop your cherry, Layla, but not until you're really mine."

He pulls away from my grasp, and I know I've lost him.

"I'll find you some clothes to wear."

With that, he disappears below deck, and I'm left to rub my stinging wrists and wonder what the hell I've agreed to.

5

SAILOR

Just knowing that Layla is sleeping in the cabin next door makes my cock hard as rock. Walking away from her swollen pussy last night was the hardest thing I've ever had to do. But I won't take her until she understands she's mine.

This morning I'm up early setting lobster traps off the back of the boat. I've got one day to convince Layla she's mine, and I don't mean to waste it.

By the time Layla comes above deck, looking gorgeous in one of my oversized t-shirts, I've got breakfast laid out and ready.

Her eyes go wide when she sees the fresh fruit platter and bottle of champagne on ice.

"Is this how you always eat?'

"Only on special occasions."

She gives me a lopsided look. "And what's the special occasion?"

I pop the champagne and pour her a glass. "It's the day you realize we're meant to be together."

Her eyes roll into the back of her head. She thinks I'm kidding, but I'm not.

I take a seat opposite her, and we sip champagne and eat mango slices while watching the morning sun sparkle on the water.

"So, what did you do before?"

"Before what?"

She sweeps her hand expansively. "Before you bought a big-ass yacht?"

I've been hesitant to tell Layla about my past. I'm not sure how much of the truth she can handle. "I worked in the city."

She sets her glass down. "Why are you so evasive?"

She's looking at me intensely, frustrated. I should tell her the truth about me, but now's not the time.

"Some other time, Layla. Today, let's have some fun."

She gives me a sideways smile and a look that makes me instantly hard. "I like the sound of that."

"Not that kind of fun." Her smile turns into a pout, which does nothing to ease my hard-on.

I get up from the table and hold out my hand. "Come on."

A half hour later she's on the back of the jet ski, clinging onto my waist. Her hair whips around me in the wind, and her laugh carries on the breeze as we speed through the water, turning to jump over our wake.

"Slow down!" she cries, but I only go faster, circling the island and coming back around to the yacht. When I pull into the dock at the back of the boat, her cheeks are rosy, her hair windswept, and there's a smile on her face.

"I thought you'd like that."

Her smile is infectious, and I find myself laughing along with her. "I'll have to pick up another one so you can ride your own."

Her look darkens. "You talk as if I'm staying, but I'll be back in Temptation Bay tomorrow."

I raise my eyebrows. "Or you could stay here with me, drink champagne for breakfast every morning, eat fresh fish, and go joyriding on a jet ski all day."

She puts a hand on her hips. "How can you afford all of this? Are you some kind of millionaire or something?"

She's close, but that's not how I want to win her over, not with money. "Not quite, honey. I just got lucky." Which is kind of the truth.

Now that we're off the water, she's shivering in her wet t-shirt.

"You should go get warm. Meet me on the deck for lunch."

The rest of the day is spent swimming and sunbathing on deck while reading books. We talk a lot. I find myself opening up to Layla in ways I haven't before.

By the time sunset comes, I realize what my body has known since I first laid eyes on her. I love Layla, and I don't want to let her go.

6

LAYLA

As the sun sets, Sailor brings out a woolen blanket and wraps it around my shoulders. We've had the best day ever. Jet skiing and swimming and talking. I can't remember the last time I laughed so much.

Sailor cooked lobster for dinner, plucked straight from the ocean. As I suck the juices off my fingers, I wonder what it would be like to live on a boat permanently and travel from place to place. Not having to worry about money, because Sailor clearly has enough of it if he owns a boat this big with room to park a jet ski or two.

I shake the thought out of my head. I'm going back home tomorrow. It's crazy to even consider staying here with a complete stranger. Especially one that kidnapped me.

But if it's so crazy, then why does it feel so right?

After dinner, I help Sailor with the dishes. The kitchen is bigger than the one in my cottage. It's got modern appliances and a well-stocked fridge humming in the corner.

Sailor told me he puts to land about every week or so for supplies but spends the rest of his time sailing down the coast.

He'll get to Mexico eventually, but why stop there? There are so many coastlines to explore.

Back on deck, Sailor hands me a mug of hot chocolate, and I wrap my hands around it, savoring the warmth.

It's dark now, and the stars are a canopy of twinkling lights above us. Away from the mainland, there're so many that my eyes can barely take it all in.

"It's beautiful, isn't it?"

Sailor sits beside me, and we both tilt our heads heavenward. His arm goes around me, and I lean into his shoulder.

As his hand slides down my arm, I feel a spark ignite within me at his touch. My mind goes back to last night and his mouth on my pussy.

I wriggle around so that I'm facing him. His mouth closes over mine, and our tongues tangle in the kiss.

My body fills with heat as his hand slides over my breasts.

In an instant, he's pulled my top off and I'm half naked in front of him. His eyes drink me in, and I feel confident under his gaze, not bothering to hide my flabby bits.

His hand slides to my panties, and he pulls them off, exposing my pussy.

But I want more than last night. I want all of him. I undo his belt, and this time he doesn't stop me. Taking his cock into my hands, I roll it along my palms.

Sailor groans, a deep guttural sound.

I slide off the couch and onto my knees before him. "What are you doing, sweetheart?"

In answer, I run my tongue around his tip and his groan deepens. My lips close around his cock and slide down his shaft as my palms cup his balls.

My mouth works his hard cock, sucking and nibbling until I feel him lengthen.

Sailor tugs on my hair, and I let his cock pop out of my mouth.

"You keep doing that and I'm gonna come."

"Would that be so bad?"

He pulls me to my feet and stands up, his cock sliding between my legs to the place where my thighs meet. My engorged pussy lips part as he slides along them, my juices coating his cock.

"Sailor," I gasp.

My entrance is on fire as he runs his cock over it, but every time I move my hips, he moves out of the way, so his cock doesn't go inside.

"Sailor," I whine. "I want you inside me."

"Are you mine?"

I'll agree to fucking anything right now, but I know what he's asking. Will I stay?

I think of the magical day we've had, all of the talking and laughing. I think of the feel of him against me. But then I think of my sister and not being there when she gets back from college.

"I don't know."

He slides his cock along my pussy lips. My whole core shudders.

"I can't fuck you until you're mine, Layla. I want your mind and soul before I take your body."

He's undoing me with his words, whispering into my neck as his cock slides between my wet folds, pressing against my nub.

I can't make him any promises. I can't give him what he wants, so he won't give me what I want.

"Fuuuck." It feels so fucking good. I rub myself against his cock, letting his hardness press into my nerve center.

His mouth closes around my nipple and I cry out. He won't fuck me, but he's got no problem letting me rub against his hard cock. The pressure builds quickly, and I cry out in surprise.

"I'm gonna come."

"Good girl. Come for me."

He's breathing hard, and as I tip over the edge, coming all over his hard cock, he stiffens and groans and hot liquid squirts onto my thighs. His hot cum shoots down my leg in thick ropes as my pussy trembles against him.

We press together, clinging together. Trembling from our joint release.

Afterwards, Sailor brings me tissues and gently wipes me clean. I'm aching to feel him inside. And I wonder what it would be like to give in. To submit and stay.

7

SAILOR

When I wake, Layla's warm body presses next to mine. Her scent fills my nostrils, and I breathe deep, breathing her in and getting high on her scent.

She stirs as I roll over, and her eyes flutter open. God she's beautiful. I could get used to waking up next to this woman every morning.

Only this is the last morning. This is the day I have to take her back.

I should get up and hoist the sails and get her back to mainland, but I don't. Instead, I pull her soft, warm body toward mine and wrap my arm firmly around her. If this is the last morning we have together, I want to make the most of it.

It's a few hours later and we're on deck. The shore has just come into view on the horizon, and it's unsettling how much it makes Layla smile.

I thought the days here with me would convince her to stay. But it seems she can't wait to get home.

We don't speak much as the shoreline gets closer. The marina comes into view along with the row of shops where I first spied my love. It was only two days ago, but it feels like we've lived a lifetime together.

I anchor the yacht close to shore, and we sit for a while watching tourists walk along the beach.

Layla's hair is windswept and unbrushed, falling in unruly waves down her back, her cheeks pink from the wind and sun.

"Layla…" We're sitting together on the deck seats, and I reach for her hand. "The moment I saw you coming out of that shop, I wanted you."

Her eyes meet mine. I read her indecision in them. I've got one last chance to convince her to stay.

"Not just your body." My eyes run over her luscious rack, and she trembles under my gaze. My cock hardens just thinking about the things we've done and all the things we haven't.

"I love you, Layla." Her eyes go wide in surprise. "I knew it the moment I saw you. You're the only woman for me. Come away with me, Layla. Sail away with me."

She bites her lip and looks down.

"I don't know, Sailor…"

"What don't you know? Don't you feel this too? This connection."

I tilt her chin up so she's forced to look at me. "This isn't usual, Layla. This feeling we've got. It only happens once in a lifetime."

Her eyes bore into mine, and I know the questions she's going to ask before she opens her mouth.

"What do you do, Sailor, or what did you do? How do you have all this money?" She indicates the boat. "This big fancy yacht. How can you even fund this lifestyle?"

I run my hand over my stubble, trying to buy some time.

If I'm asking her to come away with me, then she has a right to know the truth.

"I haven't always been an honest man, Layla."

She nods her head slowly. "I figured it might be something like that. What did you do, Sailor?"

"I used to work in a bank."

Her eyebrows shoot up into her hairline. And yeah, I bet she wasn't expecting that. I can hardly remember my life in a suit and an office.

"But it was a front. I've got buddies who are into bad stuff. There was a team of us, and we organized a heist. With my inside knowledge, we got away with it."

She pulls her hands away from mine and covers her mouth, shocked. "You're a bank robber?"

I chuckle. "No, we were much more sophisticated than that. Drilled through an outside wall and right into the safe where the lock boxes were kept. Stole jewelry, money, bonds. Millions of dollars' worth."

She shakes her head, trying to process it.

"I told you, I'm not a good man. But I only did the one job, and that was enough for me. I'm not greedy. I just wanted enough to fund a life on the water. To sail my boat around for a few years. Come back when the heat cools off."

"Are people looking for you?"

I scratch my stubble, wondering, because that's something I don't know.

I quit my job at the bank a few months before we did the job so they couldn't link it back to me. From what I've heard, the feds are still scratching their asses about the heist. But it's best to lay low for a while. Maybe for several years.

Layla's holding her head in her hands, and it's alarming. I've taken a risk telling her the truth, especially with her brother being in the Coast Guard.

But I trust my gut about Layla. She won't tell on me.

"Now you know the truth about me. The whole truth, sweetheart. Do you want to stay?"

8

LAYLA

I'm trying to understand what Sailor's telling me. He's a robber. He did a heist. The yacht, the jet skis, the champagne—it's all funded with stolen money.

It should make me run. It should be the deciding factor in not staying with him. But strangely, it doesn't bother me as much as it should. That makes me almost as bad as he is.

Only he's not all bad, is he? He's been kind to me, cooked for me, gave me orgasms. My body trembles at the memory.

But if Sailor is capable of organizing a heist, what else is he capable of?

Something occurs to me, something that hasn't sat quite right for the last two days.

"Sailor?" His eyes snap to mine at the tone. "The night we met and I drank too much..."

He looks sideways, and I know my suspicions are right.

"I didn't drink too much, did I?"

He rubs his stubble but doesn't say anything.

"I've been thinking about it. I only had two cups of coffee with whiskey in them. That's not enough to make me so drunk that I can't remember. I haven't drank much before, but I've seen my brother. He'll drink a whole bottle of whiskey and still remember."

I take a deep breath, needing to know the truth but not wanting to know it at the same time. "Did you drug me?"

He looks down, and I know the truth without him saying it.

"It was the only way to get you on my boat."

He reaches for my hand, and I pull it away.

Everything about the last two days has been a lie. His tenderness, his kindness. It was making up for the fact that he drugged me and took me.

"I knew from the moment I first saw you that you were meant to be mine." The look he gives me is hungry and intense.

Despite my anger, the words send a thrill through my body. My stupid body.

"That doesn't mean you can go around and drug any girl you want."

"No." He grabs my wrists. "You're not any girl, Layla. You're my woman, the only woman I'll ever want."

I twist my wrists and he lets go. "Stop saying that. You barely know me."

"I know enough."

"I want to go home, Sailor."

He looks at me long and hard, and I see the conflict behind his eyes.

"Very well." Without another word, he goes to the back of the boat and readies the tender. I step on board, and he ferries us to the jetty.

I don't speak to him. I can't even look at him. The man I thought was so kind and funny and tentative is nothing but a brute.

But he's your brute, my stupid heart whispers.

We get to the jetty, and I jump out before he's even tied the rope.

"I'll leave at sundown," he calls after me. "I'll wait for you 'til then."

"Don't bother waiting," I call over my shoulder. And with my heart breaking in two, I head for home.

Coraline's car is parked out front, but even seeing my happy, carefree sister doesn't lighten my mood.

Her face falls as soon as she sees me. "What's up, sis?"

There's no hiding anything from my sister.

While she makes a pot of coffee, I tell her all about Sailor, the instant attraction when I met him, the two fantastic days on the boat, and how he drugged me to kidnap me. The only thing I don't tell her is that he's a criminal on the run.

When I finish talking, there're tears streaming down my face, and she's got a consoling arm around me.

"So, what's the problem?"

I stare at her through my tear-filled eyes. "The problem? He drugged me, Coraline. He laced my drink so he could steal me away on his boat."

"Sounds kinda romantic. That he stole you away so he could prove himself to you."

I stare at her. I can't believe my strait-laced sister thinks that's romantic. "Maybe if you're a psychopath?"

"Is he?"

I think about the days we spent together. Sailor is a lot of things. A thief, a kidnapper, a man of dubious morals. But he's not a psycho. "No."

He's also funny and attentive and knows how to do amazing things with his tongue. "I felt safe with him. Like he'd do anything for me, anything to have me."

There's a faraway look in Coraline's eyes. She gives a long sigh. "I wish I had someone like that."

I sit up straight in my chair. "Where is my sister, and what have you done with her?"

Coraline's always been too focused on her studies to think about men. She's never had a boyfriend and never wanted one, as far as I know.

Something clicks.

"You've met someone!" A laugh escapes my lips because this is the best news I've heard all day.

Coraline smiles shyly, and I throw my arms around her.

"Well, we're not dating or anything, but there's someone I've got my eye on."

"Coraline, that's awesome. Is he from around here?"

She looks sideways. "Kinda"

There's something she's not telling me, but before I get the chance to pry it out of her, the door bangs open and Andrew strides in.

He takes one look at me and his face turns red with anger. "Where the hell have you been?"

I cringe at his words. "I was on a boat."

"A fucking boat? With a strange man, I bet. Yeah, that's right. Don't think you weren't seen walking around town with a man. There's not a thing that goes on in Temptation Bay that I don't know about."

"I doubt that," Coraline mutters under her breath, earning an angry look from Andrew.

"I've had to have microwave meals, and no laundry's been done. The dishes are a mess…"

So that's it. My brother was only concerned about me because he didn't have a slave to do the housework.

As he drones on, I think about the last two days and how happy I've been, how stress free. How good I feel around Sailor. He may not be perfect, but I love him.

The thought hits me like a ton of bricks, and I know instantly what I'm going to do.

Standing up from the table, I fix my brother with a serene look.

"You'll have to learn to look after yourself."

"What do you mean?" he splutters.

"That strange man everyone saw me with? I'm leaving with him."

Andrew's mouth drops open, and while he's gaping at me, I head upstairs to pack my things.

I'm throwing clothes into a bag when I hear footsteps outside the door. Probably Andrew coming to apologize and beg me to stay.

There's a rattle at the door and the sound of a key turning in the lock. I stride to the door and turn the handle, but it's too late. The door's locked.

"What are you doing?" I bang on the heavy wooden door.

Andrew's voice comes from the other side, hard and cold.

"You're not going anywhere, Layla. I'll keep you locked in if I have to."

I push at the door, throwing my shoulder against it. But it's no use. It doesn't budge. After a few attempts and with an aching shoulder, I slump to the floor, accepting the truth.

I'm locked in, and it's almost sundown.

9

SAILOR

The sunset turns the sky blood orange as I wait for Layla at the jetty.

I might have kidnapped her to get her here, but I won't force her to stay. It's got to be her decision.

But the way she left me, I'm not sure she's coming back.

Even though it was hard to say, I'm glad I told her the whole truth. She has to know what I'm capable of. What I'll do for her.

Though the thought provides little comfort as the sky darkens and the sun creeps closer to the horizon.

A cold breeze blows in off the ocean. The minutes tick past. The sky turns from orange to gray as the sun disappears below the horizon.

If she was coming, she would have been here by now.

My chest constricts, my heart aches, and I clench my fists in frustration. I had the woman I love on my boat, and I lost her.

I won't stick around in Temptation Bay. I can't. I've spent the afternoon picking up supplies and waiting on the jetty, and the locals are giving me suspicious looks. A rough, bearded man with tattoos draws too much attention.

I need to get away from here.

With a heavy heart, I unhook the rope, crank the engine, and navigate the waters in the fading light.

It's a short trip to where the yacht is anchored, and I tether the small boat and prepare to leave, all the while glancing back at the shore just in case Layla changes her mind.

My yacht seems empty without Layla. Her laugh, her smile, and the sweet taste of her pussy. I miss her. It's a dull ache in my heart.

I played my hand, and I lost. Now all I want to do is get as far away from here as possible.

It's time to go.

I'm securing the deck when I hear it—my name coming to me softly on the ocean breeze.

In an instant, I cross the deck and peer into the dim light.

"Sailor!" A figure waves from the beach, both arms flung into the air. It's her. Layla.

"Sailor, don't leave without me." The ache in my heart lifts, and it feels like my chest opens up and lets in the light. She came back.

Layla wades into the water as she calls out to me. The light is dim and that water must be cold.

"She's fucking crazy."

But I'm crazy too.

"I'm coming for you, sweetheart," I call to her as I pull off my jeans.

Then I dive into the sea. The cold water makes my head ache, but I push through it. I need to get to my girl.

With strong strokes, I pull myself closer to Layla, through the breakers and to where she's knee-deep with the waves crashing around her.

The waves push me against her, and I clutch her in both hands. "I thought you weren't coming."

She's breathless and soaking wet from the waist down.

"My brother locked me in my room. I had to climb onto the roof to get out."

"You did that for me?"

"I'd do anything to be with you. I'm yours, Sailor, all yours."

The words warm my heart and make my cock hard as rock. I crash my lips into hers, and she presses herself against me.

"Say that again, baby." My mouth moves over her throat, tasting the salty loveliness of her.

"I'm yours, all yours."

As she says it, I slide my hand up her skirt. The water's cold but her pussy's warm with a sticky wetness. I slide my hand into her panties.

"And I claim you." My finger slides into her as I say the words, making her gasp.

Her hips writhe against me, and she bears down on my palm, pushing my finger further inside her.

In the darkening light, her eyes are hooded with desire.

There're shadows of people on the beach, but I don't care. I've waited too long for this, and I need to make her mine. Now.

She seems to understand because her hands grab at my underwear, and then she's got my cock in her warm palm.

"Straddle me, sweetheart."

Her panties come off with a quick tug, and I lift her hips, the crashing waves making her light. Her thighs part and my dick nestles between her lips.

The water causes some resistance, and I push hard until my cock slides into her opening.

"Sailor," she cries, her hands gripping me tight.

"Hold on, darling. I'm gonna pop your cherry and it might hurt."

"Do it," she gasps. "Do it, Sailor."

I pull her down hard so my dick slides all the way inside her. She cries out, and her pussy clenches so tight I think I might lose it.

"Fuuck, Layla!" I roar.

The waves slap against us and we rock with them, her hips moving with the motion of the water and tugging my cock along with her.

With one hand, I hold her in place. With the other, I grab her tits, tearing her top open so I can wrap my mouth around her nipples.

They're splashed with salt water and hard under my tongue.

The waves rock us together, but it's not enough for me.

Now that I'm inside her velvety pussy, I'm overtaken by my animal instincts.

Grabbing her hips, I lift her up and down my cock, sliding her pussy along my shaft until my nerve ends are buzzing.

My balls pull up tight, and I'm so close to releasing myself into her. Layla wiggles against me and I press against her, making sure she gets friction against her clit.

"Fuck, Sailor."

"That's it, sweetheart. Let everyone know who's fucking you. Who do you belong to?"

"Sailor!" She wails, and it almost sends me over the edge.

I slam into her, and she cries my name as she comes. That's all I need. My balls explode, shooting ropes of hot cum into her pussy.

The waves crash around us, and I crash into her, exploding with a roar that they must hear all the way down the coast.

Her pussy convulses around me, milking every last drop of my seed.

Layla's mine now. Forever. I've claimed her.

A wave almost bowls us over, and we break apart. It's almost completely dark now. The boat is just a shadow looming in the bay.

"We need to go, darling. I don't want to stay here tonight. Can you swim?"

She gives me a look. "I grew up in Temptation Bay. Of course I can swim."

We leave our clothes discarded in the waves and, half naked, dive into the water. It's only a few meters to the boat, and I get up first and then pull Layla on board.

We're dripping wet and laughing as we fall exhausted onto the deck.

Layla's all mine and on my boat by choice this time. I've got my woman, and that's all I need.

EPILOGUE

LAYLA

Five years later…

The water lapping against the boat almost drowns out the cries of the baby. Almost. But not quite.

Pulling myself out of bed, I pad over to the basinet and scoop Tyler into my arms. "Shhh, little one."

I sit on the end of the bed and bounce her in my arms. Her cries get louder. "You want some milk?"

Pulling my top aside, I guide her little head to my breast, and she latches onto the nipple, sucking hungrily.

The door opens and Sailor tentatively pokes his head through. "Did you manage to get a nap?"

I nod. Even that action makes me feel weary. "Yeah, a little."

"Momma." Samson pushes past him and runs into the room, his face lit up with excitement.

"Daddy took me on the jet ski."

"Did he now?"

I give Sailor a look, but I'm not really upset. Even at three years old, Samson can swim, and Sailor would protect that boy with his life.

We thought about putting to land when we started a family. But we love our life on the water too much.

It took a bit of effort to babyproof the yacht, and it doesn't look as stylish with netting all around the edge, but it keeps our little family safe.

Both the babies were water births, so you could say they were born into it.

Even though the heat has died down around Sailor and his heist, we decided to stay on the ocean.

When Samson's old enough, I'll homeschool him, but for now, he enjoys swimming, fishing, and doing whatever his daddy does.

"We need supplies soon. You want to stop in at the next bay for a few days?"

We're somewhere along the coast of Mexico. Since we had the children, we tend to stop on land a bit more often.

"We could find you a nanny, some help with the baby?"

I shake my head. Sailor has offered this before. And even though I'm exhausted and my nipples ache—and not in a good way—I wouldn't have it any other way. I'm lucky enough that I can sleep when the baby sleeps and we don't have to work.

"No thanks. I'm fine."

Sailor sits next to me on the bed and runs his hand around my waist. He nuzzles into my neck, smiling over my shoulder as he watches Tyler feed.

"I love you." He whispers it against my neck, and my skin's instantly on fire.

A trail of kisses tickles the back of my neck. I shiver in anticipation. I know once the kids have gone to bed later, it'll be our time alone.

Sailor gets up from the bed. "I'll start dinner."

He shoots me a look. "But we're having some quiet time later."

"What's quiet time?" pipes up Samson.

"It's when mommy and daddy do something nice together."

"I want quiet time too."

We both laugh, and Sailor herds Samson out of the room. They close the door behind them, and I'm left with the quiet sound of a suckling baby.

Yeah, it's exhausting sometimes, but I wouldn't have it any other way. I have my family. I have Sailor. And that's all I need.

PROTECTING HIS BRAT

This brat needs to be taught a lesson, and I'll be the one to discipline her...

Since retiring from the special forces, I've set up a team of elite personal security guards.

But I wasn't expecting the daughter of my first client to be such a brat.

Adrianna thinks she can play me, but she needs to be taught a lesson.

I'll be the one to take her over my knee.

She needs to learn that the only game I'm playing is for keeps.

Protecting His Brat is an OTT age-gap romance featuring an older military hero and a young curvy virgin.

mybook.to/ProtectingHisBrat

GET YOUR FREE BOOK

Sign up to the Sadie King mailing list for a FREE book!

You'll be the first to hear about new releases, exclusive offers, bonus content and all my news. You can even email me back. I love chatting with my readers!

To claim your free book visit:
www.authorsadieking.com/free

BOOKS BY SADIE KING

Sunset Coast

Underground Crows MC

Sunset Security

Men of the Sea

Filthy Rich Love

The Cod Cove Trilogy

Wild Heart Mountain

Military Heroes

Mountain Heroes

Wild Riders MC

Maple Springs

Men of Maple Mountain

All the Single Dads

Candy's Café

Small Town Sisters

For a full list of titles visit the Sadie King website

www.authorsadieking.com

ABOUT THE AUTHOR

Sadie King is a USA Today Best Selling Author of short instalove romance.

She lives in New Zealand with her ex-military husband and raucous young son.

When she's not writing she loves catching waves with her son, runs along the beach, and good wine, preferably drunk with a book in hand.

Keep in touch when you sign up for her newsletter. You'll even snag yourself a free short romance!

Visit: www.authorsadieking.com/free

www.authorsadieking.com